Stumps

by

Mark Morris

First published in 2009 in Great Britain by
Barrington Stoke Ltd
18 Walker Street, Edinburgh, EH3 7LP

www.barringtonstoke.co.uk

ISBN: 978-1-84299-662-1

Printed in Great Britain by Bell & Bain Ltd

A Note from the Author

I've always loved ghost stories. My favourites are those set in lonely places far away from anywhere. Stumps grew bit by bit from a number of different ideas I had rattling round in my head.

On holiday in Cornwall once, my family and I went to a sculpture park, and saw the tips of five huge fingers, carved in wood, sticking out of the ground. It looked as though a giant hand was thrusting itself up from deep below in the earth. It made a real impact on me, and I filed away the image for future use. As for the thin, dark figure that emerges from the woods, whenever I look out over a vast stretch of land, I find myself always thinking of a nightmare figure rushing towards me, starting from far away and then suddenly being close up. I find myself wondering how I would react if such a thing were to happen in real life.

And the rest? It all simply grew from those two images – the huge hand and the thin dark figure – and I built up the story from there. The lovely neighbours in the story, though, are based on real people, our ex-neighbours, who brought my wife and me a huge box of straw-berries as a welcoming present when we moved into our last house.

For Kev
Nearly thirty years of friendship and
hundreds of movies later ...

With special thanks to our readers:
Sean Hurl
Liz Williams
Tom Redshaw
Leeann Wilkie
Suzanne Louden
Paul Carberry

Contents

Chapter 1
The Discovery

The Morgan family were in the over-grown garden of their new house, cutting down weeds and long grass. Suddenly sixteen-year-old Ellie Morgan gave a shout.

"Hey, Mum! Look at this!"

Her mother, Bridget, looked up. She pushed through the long grass to stand at her daughter's side.

"What is it?" she asked.

Ellie pointed at what she had found. It was a stump of polished wood, about three feet tall.

It was smooth and round at the top and looked like the tip of a giant finger sticking out of the ground.

Suddenly Bridget gasped.

"What is it, Mum?" Ellie asked.

"Just for a moment I thought I saw it move," Bridget said. "It must have been the sun-light across it."

Ellie put her hand on the stump. "What do you think it is?" she said.

"I don't know," Bridget replied with a shrug. "A sculpture maybe?"

Just then twelve-year-old Miles came running round the side of the house. His face was red and sweaty, and his clothes were covered in grass and dirt.

"Hey, you two, come and see what me and Dad have found," he said.

Then he saw the stump.

"Oh, wow, you've found one as well," he said.

Chapter 2
Watching the House

It took the Morgans three days to clear the garden. They had been in their new house for a week by then. They had come here from Leeds to make a fresh start. For the past year, Bridget and her husband, Colin, had been having problems in their marriage, and they hoped that the move would help them to put it all behind them.

As they had cut down the long grass in the garden, the Morgans had found more of the stumps. There were seven in all, three at the front of the house, two at the back and one at each side. Each of the stumps stood about three feet tall and was made of the same dark, polished wood. Bridget had looked out of the kitchen window at the back of the house several times during the past few days, and each time she had jumped, thinking that the stumps were small figures, crouching down in the grass.

It was now evening, and the family were sitting around the fire in their front room.

"I think they were put there to watch the house," said Ellie.

"What a creepy idea," Bridget said with a shudder.

"No," said Ellie, "I mean in a good way. They look after the house while we're asleep."

"You mean they're looking over us?" said Colin. He was staring into the fire and the flames were reflected in his eyes.

"Yes," said Ellie, and at that moment a chunk of wood burst in the fire, and a shower of sparks flew up the chimney, making them all jump.

Chapter 3
Hidden

Bridget woke up with a jolt. It took her a moment to work out that it was dark and she was in bed. She couldn't think what had woken her. A dream, maybe. Then from over by the window she heard a creak.

She sat up and turned on the light. Colin was sitting by the window, staring out into the darkness.

"What are you doing?" she asked.

He looked tired, but he said, "I couldn't sleep. Too much on my mind."

"Like what?" she asked.

He gave a shrug. After a moment he said, "Did we do the right thing coming here, Bridget?"

"Of course we did!" she said. "It's a beautiful place and the kids love it. It'll take a lot of doing up, but we've got all the time in the world. I love you, Colin."

"I love you too," he said with a smile. Then his face fell. "It scares me to think I nearly lost you."

She got out of bed, crossed the room and hugged him. "No one's going to lose anyone," she said.

They stayed there, clinging to each other for a moment. Then Colin said, "They weren't here before."

"What weren't?" asked Bridget.

"The stumps," he said. "They weren't here the first time we came to look at the house."

"They must have been," said Bridget.

"No, I'm sure they weren't. We walked all the way round the house, through the long grass. We didn't see a single one."

"They must have been hidden, that's all," said Bridget.

Then she felt a shiver run through her.

"Come back to bed," she said.

Chapter 4

Neighbours

The next day, Bridget had finished painting the walls in the hall-way and was cleaning the brushes when there was a knock on the front door. She left the brushes sitting in water and went to open it.

Standing outside were a man and a woman about the same age as her and Colin. The man was tall and wore a T-shirt, shorts and sandals. The woman was plump and wore a yellow dress and large sun-glasses. The woman was holding a basket of strawberries.

"Hello," the man said with a smile. "We're your new next-door neighbours. I'm Tom and this is my wife, Claire. We live about half a mile away over there." He pointed to his left.

"We've brought you a house-warming present," Claire said, holding up the basket of strawberries.

"Oh, how kind of you!" Bridget said. She looked at her watch. "We're just about to stop for lunch. Why don't you stay too? I'll give the others a shout."

Half an hour later, the four adults, plus Ellie and Miles, were sitting out in the back garden, eating strawberries and cream.

Tom and Claire's surname was Woodall, and they had two children, a daughter of fifteen and a son of eleven. Tom was an accountant and Claire worked part-time as a nurse at the local health centre.

They had been chatting for a while when Colin pointed at one of the stumps. "Have you any idea what these things are?" he said.

Tom shook his head. "No idea. Odd little critters, aren't they?"

"When I first looked at it, I thought it had a face," Claire said, "but I can't see it now."

"Have you any idea how long they have been here?" Colin asked.

"Or who made them?" Bridget added.

Tom gave a shrug. "No. I can't say I've ever seen them before."

"Not even the ones at the front?" asked Colin. "Not even when the last owners were here, before the grass grew long enough to cover them."

"No," said Tom, "sorry."

Colin turned to Bridget with an 'I told you so' look on his face.

"That doesn't mean they weren't here," Bridget said. "The hedge is high at the front. You wouldn't be able to see them if you were driving or walking past."

Colin gave a scowl.

Bridget asked, "Did you know Mr and Mrs Brook very well, Claire?"

The Brooks were the last owners of the house. Jean Brook, who was in her eighties, had moved out two years ago after her husband, Harry, died.

"Not really," Claire said. "I've got to know Jean better since she moved into the village. I pop in now and again to see how she is."

"Harry wasn't very welcoming," said Tom. "In fact, he was a bit of a bugger."

"In what way?" asked Bridget.

Tom and Claire looked at each other. Then Tom said, "I don't like to speak ill of the dead, but Harry was a bully."

"He used to beat poor Jean black and blue," Claire said. "Often I would see her with bruises on her face or arms."

She looked at Ellie and Miles, who had finished their strawberries now and were playing frisbee at the bottom of the garden. In a low voice she said, "And there was all sorts of gossip about him lusting after young girls. He wasn't a nice man at all."

Colin had listened to all of this without speaking. Now he said, "I wonder if it was Harry Brook who had these things made."

"What with him being such a dirty old man, it wouldn't surprise me," said Claire.

"They do look a bit rude, don't they?" said Bridget.

"Maybe they're fertility symbols," Colin said. "Maybe it's nothing to do with ..." His voice trailed off.

"To do with what?" asked Bridget.

"Oh, nothing," said Colin. "I was going to say, maybe they're not watching over us at all."

He smiled and Bridget smiled back, but she felt a little uneasy. Maybe she was being silly, but she couldn't shake off the feeling that there was something Colin wasn't telling her.

Chapter 5
The Dream

Three hours later, Bridget was lying on her bed with a cool flannel over her eyes. The smell of paint and the hot summer sun had given her a head-ache.

She fell asleep, and had a dream that she was getting out of bed and walking over to the window. The view from the window showed the back garden down below, a dirt track that ran along the back of their property, and then a huge corn field, which went back almost as far as the horizon. On the far side of the corn field, half a mile away, was a wood. From where Bridget was standing, the wood looked like nothing but a dark green mass.

All at once she saw a tiny black figure come out of the wood. Although the figure looked no bigger than an ant, Bridget knew that it was a person. She watched as the figure moved away from the wood and through the corn field, towards the house.

Although she wasn't sure why, the figure made her shiver. She knew straight away that there was something wrong with it. It was far too thin, for one thing, and it seemed to be dressed in black rags, which flapped around its body. Also it moved with a strange, lurching limp, as if one of its legs was shorter than the other.

The figure was about half-way across the field when Colin entered the back garden. As though it had seen him, or could sense him, the figure seemed to speed up. Bridget tried to bang on the glass to warn her husband, but suddenly found she couldn't move or speak.

She could only watch as Colin walked across to the nearest stump and raised his hands, as though warming himself by the fire-side.

As soon as Colin touched the stump, the hobbling figure became a blur of movement. It reached the fence at the bottom of the field and climbed over it with monkey-like ease. In an instant it had crossed the lane, entered the garden and was rushing towards her husband.

It was Colin's screams that told Bridget she had been dreaming. Her eyes flew open and she sat up, the damp flannel slipping into her lap. She leaped out of bed, ran down the stairs and dashed out into the garden.

Colin was lying at the base of the stump he had placed his hands upon in her dream. When Bridget reached him, he was whimpering like an animal, his eyes wide and wild.

"Colin!" she shouted, but he didn't respond.

Ellie and Miles ran out of the house. "What's happening, Mum?" Ellie said. "What's wrong with Dad?"

Bridget turned and said, "Miles, go inside, dial 999 and ask for an ambulance. Can you remember the address?"

Miles nodded, looking scared, and ran back into the house.

The ambulance arrived twenty minutes later. By that time Bridget had put a blanket round her husband and had checked his vital signs. She had even looked him over for bites and cuts and stings, but hadn't been able to find anything to explain why he was lying on the ground, staring into space and not responding to her or the children.

The nearest hospital was ten miles away through twisting country lanes. Bridget, Ellie and Miles followed the ambulance in the car.

"Dad will be all right, won't he, Mum?" Miles asked.

"Let's hope so," Bridget replied.

As soon as they got to the hospital, the ambulance men rushed Colin away. Bridget led the children to the waiting area, where they sat on hard seats for the next four hours. Bridget drank cup after cup of coffee, and Ellie and Miles ate crisps and chocolate from the vending machine. It was dark outside by the time a young, white-coated doctor came across to them and said, "Mrs Morgan?"

"Yes," Bridget said.

"I'm Dr Irwin," said the doctor. "We've carried out every test we can think of on your husband, and I'm pleased to report that we can find nothing wrong with him. His heart's fine, his blood pressure's normal, and there's nothing in his system that shouldn't be there. We've checked his brain activity and that's fine too. We're still waiting for the results of a few tests, but there's no reason why Colin can't go back home with you now."

"Is he awake?" Bridget asked.

"Oh, yes," said Dr Irwin. "He's sitting up and chatting away."

"Did he say what happened?" asked Ellie.

Dr Irwin smiled at her. "He says he can't remember. The last thing he remembers before waking up in hospital is being out in the garden."

"What do *you* think happened to him, doctor?" Bridget asked.

Dr Irwin frowned. "It's hard to say. We're looking into whether it could be epilepsy or some kind of panic attack, but we haven't found any evidence of either. We do know that it's not heart-related, it's not an insect bite, it's not drugs and it's not diabetes." He spread his hands. "Hopefully it'll just be a one-off. The best thing to do is go home and forget it ever happened."

"And what if it happens again?" Bridget asked.

"Let's cross that bridge if and when we come to it," Dr Irwin said.

Chapter 6
A Little Accident

Bridget's best friend, Ruth, arrived from London the next day. Ruth had promised to help Bridget choose lighting and fabrics for her new home. Ruth's visit had been planned weeks ago, and Bridget had been really looking forward to it. Now, though, because of what had happened to Colin yesterday, she was almost wishing that the visit could have been put off for a week or so.

It would have been OK if Colin had been back to normal, but the truth was, he was still acting a bit weird. He had been too tired to speak to Bridget last night when they got back from the hospital, and had gone straight to bed. And this morning she had woken up to find him lying beside her with his hands covered in bandages.

"Colin," she said, giving him a nudge.

He had groaned and turned away from her.

"Come on, Colin, please talk to me," she said. "You still haven't told me what happened yesterday."

He had opened one eye and looked at her. "Can't remember," he muttered.

"Why have you put bandages on your hands?" she asked him.

"They hurt," he said.

"Why do they hurt?"

He frowned. "I don't know."

"Do you remember putting your hands on one of the stumps yesterday?" she asked.

He went very still for a moment. Then he shook his head. "No."

"Describe the pain in your hands," she said.

"Hot. Stinging. Burning." Then he closed his eyes again. "Very tired. Just want to sleep."

"All right," she sighed. "You go back to sleep. But if there's something wrong, you tell me. No secrets, remember."

Ruth arrived at noon. Colin was still in bed by then. Bridget told Ruth that he had a bug, but Bridget wasn't sure that Ruth believed her. Apart from herself and Colin, Ruth was the only other person who knew the full story of what had happened last year. She knew that Colin had gone into a deep depression after losing his job, and that the problems this had led to between Bridget and himself had driven Bridget into the arms of Jason Riley, who worked with her at the local fitness centre.

25

It wasn't until the two women were sitting out in the garden, having coffee, mid-way through the afternoon, that Ruth said, "So tell me what's *really* wrong."

"What do you mean?" Bridget said, trying not to look guilty.

"Oh, come on, Bridget," said Ruth. "I've known you for long enough to tell when you're hiding something."

Bridget gave a deep sigh. "It's not what you're thinking. It's nothing to do with what went on last year."

"So what is it, then?" Ruth asked.

"It's just that ... well, something odd happened yesterday," said Bridget. "I didn't tell you about it because ... well, it just sounds so weird."

"I like weird," Ruth said with a smile.

And so Bridget told Ruth everything, and after that she felt better for having done so.

When she had finished, Ruth looked back towards the distant woods with a shudder. "Do you really think there's something up there?"

"No, I don't," said Bridget firmly.

"So what do you think happened, then?" Ruth asked.

"I think I had a bad dream and my mind started playing tricks with me," Bridget said.

Ruth looked at the nearest stump. "Do you dare me to touch it?"

"Oh, now you're being silly!" Bridget said, but all the same she looked back at the corn field and the woods beyond, remembering the impossible speed at which the thin, hobbling figure had moved in her dream.

Ruth walked over to the stump and placed her hands on it. Nothing happened.

"Happy now?" said Bridget.

"A bit let down," Ruth admitted.

Bridget picked up the empty coffee mugs and the two women went back into the house. They entered the kitchen – and stopped dead.

Colin was standing there, swaying from side to side. He looked ill, his eyes dull and glazed. He was wearing his dressing gown, but it was hanging open and he was naked beneath it.

Bridget heard Ruth gasp behind her. She said, "Jesus, Colin!" and took a step towards her husband.

Colin's face twisted with anger. "Was it him?" he snarled. "It was, wasn't it? You're all plotting against me."

He made a lunge at his wife. Shocked, Bridget jumped back, banging heads with Ruth. The sudden pain made her drop the mugs, which smashed on the floor.

Colin's bare foot came down on a jagged piece of broken mug. He screamed in pain and fell forward. He landed on more chunks of broken mug. His chin hit the floor, almost knocking him out. He lay there, his eyelids fluttering.

"Oh, God, Colin," Bridget said, and leant over him.

Behind her Ruth was groaning. She had a lump above her eyebrow that was already turning purple.

"Oh, shit, Ruth, sorry," Bridget said.

"Wasn't your fault," Ruth muttered.

Bridget ran some cold water on a cloth and gave it to Ruth to press against her head. Then she tried to lift Colin, but he was a dead weight.

"Try pouring some water on his face," Ruth said. "That might bring him round."

Bridget couldn't think of a better idea. She crossed to the sink, grabbed a mug off the draining board and filled it with water.

"Hang on, though," said Ruth. "What if he's like he was a moment ago? All sort of crazy and wild?"

"I'm not leaving him lying on all these bits of broken mug," Bridget said.

She poured water on his head. It trickled down his face. After a few seconds, his eyes snapped open. His mouth opened too as he cried out in pain.

"It's OK," Bridget breathed, and began to stroke his head. "I'm here."

Colin's eyes focused on her. "What's happening?" he mumbled.

"You've had a little accident," Bridget said, "but you'll be OK. Can you move?"

"Dunno," Colin said. His face creased in pain. "It really hurts."

"You've got to push yourself up on your arms if you can," Bridget said. "Come on, I'll help you."

Ruth came over to help and they slowly got Colin to his feet. Bits of broken mug were stuck in his stomach and chest, but there wasn't as much blood as Bridget had feared. They sat him down, and Bridget spent the next few minutes tending to her husband's wounds and clearing up the mess of broken crockery and spilled blood. Most of Colin's cuts were small, but a few pottery splinters had embedded themselves so deeply into his flesh that Bridget had to pry them free with tweezers. The gash in Colin's foot was the worst of the injuries. Bridget cleaned and disinfected it and bandaged it up.

When all that was done, Bridget and Ruth helped Colin up to bed. He was dazed and looked white as a sheet, and he sank back into his pillows with a groan. As soon as the two women were back downstairs, Bridget started to shake. Ruth, who now had a large plaster above her eye, made them both a cup of tea.

Sipping from her mug, Ruth said, "What was all that about?"

"I don't know," Bridget said in a dull voice. "He must have been having a bad dream."

Ruth was silent for a moment. Then she said, "What do you think would have happened if I hadn't been here?"

"What do you mean?" said Bridget.

Ruth gave her a grim look. "If we hadn't banged heads together and you hadn't dropped the mugs, Colin would have attacked you."

"Don't be silly," said Bridget, but she looked away.

"You've got to face facts," said Ruth. "You were lucky that I was around. Colin is ill, Bridget. He needs to see someone. You need to take him back to the hospital."

All at once Bridget began to weep.

"Hey," Ruth said, putting her arms around her friend, "don't cry. The doctors will find out what's wrong with him. Everything will be all right."

"What if it isn't?" sobbed Bridget. "What if they take him away from us and lock him up somewhere?"

"They won't," Ruth said, but she didn't sound sure.

The two women were silent for a moment. Then Ruth said, "What do you think Colin meant when he said 'Was it him'? Who's 'him', do you think?"

Bridget thought again of the dark, hobbling figure moving towards her husband at an incredible speed. She gave a shudder.

"I don't know," she said.

Chapter 7
Digging

Bridget was drunk. Over dinner that evening she and Ruth had worked their way through several bottles of wine. She remembered kissing Ellie and Miles goodnight around 9.30, and the next thing she knew she was waking up in the darkness with her head pounding.

She lay in bed for a few moments, trying to work out what had woken her. She felt as though it had been some kind of sound, though all was silent now.

"Colin," she said in a whisper, and reached out a hand in the darkness. Colin was not beside her. There was a warm hollow in the bed where he had been.

Her head felt as though it was full of wet clay, but she made herself sit up. She didn't feel well, but her need to find out if Colin was OK was stronger than her need to sleep off her hangover. She took several deep breaths, and then stood up and padded out on to the landing in her bare feet.

The house was silent and dark. Not wishing to wake Ruth or the children, she leaned over the banister and hissed, "Colin, are you down there?"

When no answer came back she tip-toed down the stairs. At the bottom she became aware that a cold breeze from the back of the house was making her white nightshirt blow around her knees. She hurried along the landing and into the kitchen, and saw that the back door was standing open. Stopping just

35

long enough to drag on a jacket and a pair of trainers, she went out into the garden.

The fresh air was cold, but it made her feel a bit better. There was a big fat moon in the sky, throwing silver light on to the land below.

"Colin," Bridget called again, "are you out here?"

Once more there was no reply, but Bridget could make out a dark shape moving in the corn field across the road. Thinking of the lopsided figure, she felt a jolt of fear, but then she saw that the shape was moving away from her, not towards her. She hurried down the garden, past the stumps crouching like trolls. She went through the gate, across the dirt track and climbed over the wooden fence into the corn field.

The figure ahead of her was over half-way across the field, not far from the edge of the wood.

"Colin!" Bridget called again, but the figure kept on going.

She set off through the field, the corn stalks scraping against her legs. As the figure reached the dark mass of trees at the top of the field, Bridget shouted her husband's name as loudly as she could. But once again the figure neither stopped nor looked around, and an instant later it had been swallowed by the trees.

"Shit," Bridget said, and ran as fast as she could. She reached the trees and peered between them. All she could see ahead of her was blackness. She listened hard and heard the sound of rustling.

In a nervous voice she called, "Colin, are you there?"

She was answered by a burst of rustling, which made her jump. Her heart began to beat fast, then slowed down bit by bit. It must have been an animal or a bird, she thought. She told herself there was nothing to be afraid of and stepped into the wood.

Ten minutes later she was lost, and on the point of panic. Now and again a beam of moon-light would creep through the tangle of branches over-head, but most of the time it was pitch black. Bridget slipped on mud, blundered into spiky bushes, which tore at her clothes, and bumped her already throbbing head on low branches. She shouted Colin's name over and over, but there was no reply.

At last she made herself stop and listen. She was breathing hard by this time, and covered in cuts and bruises. All around her she could hear rustling. *Just the wind*, she thought. And then, beneath the rustling, she heard another sound – a sort of *thunk*-scrape, *thunk*-scrape ...

It was the sound of someone digging.

It was coming from her left. Bridget felt her heart speeding up again. She wondered whether she should find out what the sound was, or if she should just turn around and run. She could think of only one reason why someone would be digging in the middle of a wood in the dead of night. But could someone *really* be burying a body? And if so, surely it couldn't be Colin?

Although she was terrified, Bridget knew she couldn't ignore the sound. She crept towards it, trying to stay quiet, hoping she wouldn't step on a dry twig and give herself away.

The sound grew louder, but Bridget still couldn't see anything. She peered ahead, but saw only blackness. She crept closer still, clenching her teeth as leaves crackled beneath her feet. Just as she felt she must be no more than a few metres away from the sound, it stopped.

Bridget froze. Had the digger heard her, or seen the glimmer of her white nightshirt through the trees? Although she couldn't see him, she could imagine him rising slowly and turning her way. In her mind he was huge and ape-like and powerful.

Slowly she began to back away. After six or eight steps she turned and started to push her way through the trees and bushes. She felt panic rising in her. She could picture some psycho armed with a spade stalking her through the woods. Maybe he was just behind her, raising the spade to bring it crashing down on her head ...

Suddenly her foot slipped on a patch of wetness and she fell.

Her elbow hit something hard on the ground, a tree branch or a rock, and sent pain shooting through her arm. For a few minutes she could only lie there, the breath knocked from her body, waves of pain flowing through her. If there was a psycho behind her, she was now at his mercy. She listened, expecting to hear the sound of crunching foot-steps, but all was silent.

At last she climbed painfully to her feet. All she wanted to do now was get out of the woods and go home. She thought that if she walked in a straight line she would, in the end, reach the edge of the woods. And so for the next ten minutes she walked slowly forward in what she hoped was a straight line, one hand held out in front of her.

Finally she came to a thick clump of trees. She walked forward slowly, wondering if she could force her way through them. Her out-stretched hand pushed aside branches and clumps of leaves. Then it skimmed across the rough bark of a tree and touched human hair.

She sprang back with a scream. Although it was dark she saw a glint of moon-light reflected in the eyes of the person standing in front of her. She clenched her fists, and was about to scream again when a voice said, "Bridget?"

It was Colin. Bridget was so surprised that she could only gasp out her husband's name.

"Bridget," Colin said softly, "what are you doing here?"

Bridget sagged against her husband. He caught her and put his arms around her.

"I was looking for you," she said in a weak voice. "I followed you from the house. Why did you come here, Colin?"

She felt him shake his head. "I don't know," he said. "For the past two days it's like I've been sleep-walking. I must have banged my head on a branch or something. I woke up flat on my back with my foot hurting like hell. I wandered round for a bit and then I saw something white through the trees. I followed it, but it kept moving away. It turns out it was you."

She looked up at him, but couldn't see his face in the darkness. "Were you digging?" she asked.

She felt his body stiffen.

"Digging?" he repeated, and gave a little laugh. "No. Why would I do that?"

"I don't know," said Bridget. "I heard someone digging, that's all."

"Well, it wasn't me," said Colin, "not unless I was doing it in my sleep. Although with these hands I don't think so." He held out his bandaged hands. "They're still sore from whatever I did to them the other day."

"That means there must be someone else in the woods with us," said Bridget, her eyes growing wide with fear.

Colin was silent for a moment. Then he said, "Or maybe you heard an animal burrowing. Anyway, there's not much we can do about it now, is there?"

"I suppose not," said Bridget.

"Come on, then," said Colin. "Let's get out of here."

Chapter 8
Dark Days

Ruth left the next day.

"Are you sure you'll be all right?" she said to Bridget.

Bridget nodded firmly. "I'll be fine. Now stop fussing. I've told you, Colin's a lot better this morning."

As if to prove it, Colin came out of the house in shorts and a T-shirt. He was limping and his hands were still bandaged, but he did look much better.

"You just off?" he said, smiling at Ruth.

Ruth looked at him oddly. "Yes," she said.

"Well, goodbye," said Colin. "Have a safe journey home. See you soon. And ... er, sorry again about yesterday."

He gave her a hug and went back into the house.

"See?" said Bridget.

"I still think you should get him checked over," muttered Ruth.

Bridget laughed. "He's not a dog."

She hadn't told Ruth about what had happened in the woods last night, and had worn jeans and a long-sleeved top this morning to hide the scratches and bruises on her arms and legs.

Before Ruth could say anything else, Ellie and Miles came out to say goodbye. They each gave Ruth a hug, and then they watched as she got into her car and drove away, all of them waving until she was out of sight.

Bridget spent the rest of the morning chipping away the horrible tiles in the bathroom. She knew Ruth didn't really think that Colin was better, and that made Bridget cross. It seemed to her almost as if Ruth didn't *want* Colin to be well.

In some ways it was Ruth's fault that Bridget had had the affair with Jason Riley in the first place. Ruth had always been a bit jealous of Bridget's fitness, and one weekend, when Ruth had been visiting them in Leeds, the two women had gone to the Turkish baths in Harrogate together. They had been sitting side by side in the steam room when Ruth had said, "I don't believe it! You've got love handles!"

"No, I haven't!" Bridget had said.

"Yes, you have – look." And Ruth had reached out and pinched an inch of flesh above Bridget's left hip.

Because of that, Bridget had begun to spend more time working out with Jason at the fitness centre where she worked, and one thing had led to another. She was only grateful, looking back, that more people hadn't found out about the affair.

As soon as Colin found out that she and Jason were sleeping together, Jason had vanished. He had sent a letter of resignation in to work, and then had made no attempt to contact Bridget afterwards. At first she had been upset about that, but later she had thought it was for the best.

Those had been dark days, but at least some good had come out of them. The affair had given Colin the kick up the back-side he had needed to shake himself out of his depression, and it had proved to Bridget that her marriage was strong enough to withstand the problems they had faced.

And now, she thought firmly, here they were. They were making a fresh start and everything was fine.

She washed her hands and thought she'd make some sandwiches for lunch. She, Colin and the children could eat them in the garden, a proper, happy family, enjoying the sunshine and each other's company.

She was coming down the stairs when the telephone rang. It was Claire, their new neighbour, inviting Bridget round for coffee that afternoon.

"I've got a better idea," Bridget said. "Why don't you all come for a barbecue later? It would give the kids a chance to meet each other."

Claire said that they would love to, and Bridget went into the kitchen in a cheerful mood. She took the bread out of the bread bin and turned to get a knife from the knife block.

But the knife block was empty.

Normally the block held twelve knives, but now there wasn't a single one to be seen.

Puzzled, she looked in the sink, the drawers and the dish-washer, with no luck.

"What are you doing, Mum?" asked Miles, walking into the kitchen.

"Have you any idea where my knives have gone, Miles?" Bridget asked.

Miles gave a shrug. "No. I'm sure they were there last night."

Bridget felt uneasy. "See if you can find something to cut the bread with," she said. "I just want to check something."

She went out into the back garden and walked down to the old shed. She opened the shed door and went inside. The place was full of dust and cobwebs. Some of the webs had big spiders sitting in them.

It only took Bridget a few seconds to look around and confirm her fears. She walked back to the house, telling herself that just because the spade was gone, it didn't mean that Colin had taken it. And even if he had, that didn't mean he had been lying to her last night. Maybe he *had* been sleep-digging. And maybe if she went up into the woods and found the spade, she would find nothing beside it but a big empty hole.

She told herself that the reason she wasn't ready to check out the woods right now was simply because she had too many other things to do. It had nothing at all to do with the fact that she was too scared to face the truth.

Chapter 9
The Barbecue

By the time Claire, Tom and their children showed up for the barbecue later that afternoon, Bridget had told herself that she had over-reacted. She suspected that Colin *had* taken the spade and the knives into the woods last night, despite what he said. However, she told herself that he had only done it because his illness had made him confused. There was nothing more to be read into her husband's actions.

Colin was all right now, and that was the most important thing. He and Tom were standing over the sizzling meat on the barbecue, drinking beer and chatting. The children were getting along well too, and were playing badminton at the bottom of the garden. Bridget and Claire were sitting in deck-chairs, sipping wine and enjoying the sunshine.

"Grub up," Colin called, and everyone filled their plates with chicken, sausages, salad and French bread. When the food had been eaten and the plates cleared away, Ellie went indoors with Tom and Claire's daughter, Samantha, to play music, while their son, Will, played football with Miles at the bottom of the garden.

The adults re-filled their glasses and sank back into their deck-chairs. The conversation flowed easily between them. After a while, full of food and warmed by the sunshine, Bridget felt her eyes drifting closed.

"Are we boring you?" Claire said.

Bridget snapped awake. "No, sorry. I'm just tired. I didn't sleep well last night."

Tom chuckled. "Leave the poor girl alone, Claire," he said. "Let her snooze if she wants to."

Claire smiled, and was about to reply when Colin made them all jump by leaping up out of his chair.

"*What do you think you're doing?*" he screamed. "*Get your bloody hands off that!*"

For a few seconds everyone was silent, shocked by his sudden rage. Even the birds seemed to stop singing. Bridget looked at her husband and felt a wave of coldness wash through her. Colin looked like a stranger. His face was red, his teeth were clenched in a snarl, and there was a crazy look in his eyes.

She turned to see what had made him so angry. Will was leaning against the stump at the bottom of the garden, his hands pressed against its polished surface. At once Bridget saw what must have happened. The football had rolled into the slight hollow at the base of the stump and become stuck there. Will had run over to get it, and had put his hands on the stump to steady himself while he rolled the ball backwards with the sole of his foot.

Colin was marching towards him now, his arms swinging. *"Didn't you bloody hear me?"* he yelled. *"I said get your hands off that!"*

Will stared at him, frozen like a rabbit in head-lights. Colin reached the boy, grabbed his arm and yanked him away from the stump. He did it with such force that Will swung through the air and hit the ground hard enough to make his legs buckle. He lay there, his eyes wide with shock and his lips trembling as he tried not to cry.

Bridget was the first to react. She jumped up and ran across to her husband.

"What are you doing? What the hell's wrong with you?" she shouted.

Colin looked at her. His face was still twisted with anger, but his eyes were oddly blank. At that moment Bridget knew that he wasn't better, after all. Whatever was wrong with him had simply been hiding, and now it had come out again, like a crab scuttling out from under a rock.

Colin's words were like bullets. "You saw what he did. He touched that awful *thing*."

Before Bridget could reply, Tom was suddenly beside her.

"How dare you touch my son like that!" he shouted at Colin. "I ought to knock your bloody block off!"

Colin stared at Tom as if he couldn't understand the other man's anger. Shaking his head, he said, "Didn't you see what he did? Don't you people *care*?"

Bridget saw Tom clenching his fists and quickly stepped between the two men. Trying to keep her voice calm, she said, "So what if

Will touched the stump, Colin? It's just a lump of wood."

Colin looked at her in horror. "Don't you people understand anything?" Then suddenly his eyes narrowed. "No, that's not it, is it? You're all in this together. You've planned this all along."

Before Bridget could ask Colin what he was talking about, Miles darted in front of her. He looked as angry as his father had done a few moments before.

"Look what you did to Will!" Miles shouted. "You made him cry!"

Will was being comforted by Claire, who was holding him in her arms.

Colin, however, didn't even look at Will. He said, "He touched that evil ..."

"So what?" Miles shouted before his father could finish. "Like Mum says, it's just a stupid lump of wood." He ran over to the stump and put his hands on it. "See? See?"

Colin let out a roar like an animal and made a lunge at his son.

"*No!*" screamed Bridget, and leaped on to her husband's back. She was able to slow him down enough for Tom to jump in front of him and place a hand on his chest.

"No, you don't," Tom said. "You're not hurting anyone else today."

Still standing by the stump, Miles shouted, "What's wrong with you, Dad? Why can't you just be *normal?*"

Suddenly he burst into tears and ran towards the house.

Colin turned his head to watch him go.

"Don't think you can hide behind the boy," he called after his son. "Don't think I don't know who you really are."

Chapter 10
The Intruder

It was four o'clock in the morning. Bridget was lying on the settee in front of the ash-filled fire-place. She was exhausted, but she couldn't sleep. Her mind kept going over the events of the past day.

What had Colin meant when he had said *'Don't think I don't know who you really are?'* She wondered whether it was even worth trying to make sense of her husband's ravings. She hadn't been able to ask Colin, because right after saying those words, his legs had buckled, his eyes had rolled up in his head and he had passed out.

Claire had examined him lying there on the lawn and had told Bridget she thought Colin had had some kind of fit. Bridget had been close to panic, but Claire had calmly taken control. She had told Bridget she would look after things at the house while Tom drove Bridget and Colin to the hospital. And so they had laid Colin on the back seat of Tom's car, and Bridget had sat with him, her husband's head resting in her lap, while Tom drove.

Colin had looked so peaceful lying there, almost as if he was having an afternoon nap. His breathing had been normal and his colour had been good. Bridget had stroked his hair, wishing she knew what was wrong with him.

"Has anything like this happened before?" Tom asked her.

"Only in the last few days," Bridget said.

When Tom asked her what she meant, she told him everything that had happened since she had heard Colin screaming in the garden two days ago – everything, that was, apart from the 'dream' she had had just before the first 'attack'. She didn't want Tom to think she was crazy too.

"Why do you think the stumps affect him so badly?" Tom asked.

"I don't know," said Bridget.

"You should get rid of them," Tom said.

Bridget nodded. "We will. Although I'd like to find out why they were put there in the first place."

"Why don't you go and see Jean?" suggested Tom. "I'm sure Claire would go with you."

"Maybe I will," said Bridget and looked down at her husband's face. "He's so peaceful now. It's weird how this thing comes and goes. It's like he's suddenly taken over by something evil."

"By old Harry, you mean?" said Tom with a chuckle.

Bridget looked at him. "Why do you say that?"

Tom gave a shrug. "No reason. I was just thinking that maybe Harry put those things in the garden. Maybe they're evil totems or something."

Then he saw her alarmed face in the rear view mirror. "Hey, I'm joking," he said. "Ignore me. I'm an idiot."

They got to the hospital to find that Claire had phoned ahead and that Dr Irwin was waiting for them. He examined Colin and said he'd like to keep him in overnight.

Tom drove Bridget back home. When they got there, Claire suggested that Bridget, Ellie and Miles should spend the night at their house. Bridget let the children go, but said that she would rather have some time alone to think.

Nothing Claire could say would change her mind. In the end Claire said, "Well, give us a call if you want to come over later. We're only down the road."

Now Bridget was beginning to wish that she had taken Claire up on her offer. Alone in the house, she couldn't help thinking of all the darkness around her. She thought of the black field behind the house, and the even blacker woods beyond it. She thought of the hobbling, stick-thin figure in her dream. And she thought of how the light from her house would shine like a torch in the night, lit up brightly for whoever or whatever might want to pay her a visit.

She felt a shiver run through her and drew up her knees. It would be getting light soon. There was no point in going to bed. She closed her eyes, thinking that she was too on edge to sleep. The next thing she knew, she was jerking awake.

She had heard something. A scratching sound. Or had she only dreamt it? She sat up, listening – and heard a noise that made her jump.

It wasn't a scratching this time, it was a thump, as though a door was opening or closing. Bridget felt a cool breeze around her ankles. It reminded her of last night. Had someone left the back door open?

But who? She was alone in the house. Her first thought was to crawl behind the settee and hide. But she knew she couldn't just leave it. If someone – or something – was in the house with her, she needed to know.

She stood up and walked over to the sitting room door. Her heart was thumping hard and her mouth was dry. She opened the door, poked her head out into the dark hall-way and looked around. Seeing nothing, she crossed the hall-way and turned on the light.

She peered up the stairs. The shadows were a brownish colour up on the second floor landing and the door to Miles's bedroom was standing slightly open. However the breeze she could feel was coming from the kitchen at the back of the house. Taking a deep breath, she walked along the corridor at the side of the stairs that led to the kitchen.

The kitchen door was also ajar. Bridget pushed it all the way open. She stepped quickly inside and put out her left hand to the light switch on the wall. She clicked the light on and checked the room, her eyes darting everywhere.

The door that led into the back garden was closed and locked, but the window above the sink was wide open. Bridget stared at it. Had she opened it before and forgotten about it? She didn't think so. She crossed to it and leaned out to grab the edge of the frame in order to pull it closed.

As she did so, her eye was caught by something in the garden. It was too dark to see clearly, but she was sure she could see a movement on the ground, at the base of the stump that was closest to the house. She stared at the patch of blackness, but she couldn't work out whether something was struggling feebly, like a child trapped in quicksand, or whether her eyes were playing tricks on her. She blinked and looked again. This time she saw nothing at all.

She closed the window with a shudder. To put her mind at rest she would have to check the house from top to bottom. She started on the ground floor, turning on lights as she went. When she had checked every room she turned on the landing light and went upstairs, making no attempt to stifle her footsteps.

She checked Miles's room first, looking in the wardrobe and under his bed. Then she checked Ellie's room, the toilet, and the room which she intended to turn into a fitness room, which contained her exercise bike, rowing machine and weights.

When she was happy, she checked the rooms on the next floor, which included her and Colin's bedroom, the bathroom and the spare room where Ruth had stayed. These too were empty of intruders. The only room now left to check was the attic room that Colin was using as his study.

The stairs up to the attic room were steep and narrow. The door was slightly open and creaked when Bridget pushed it. She reached in and clicked the light switch, but nothing happened. It was only then that she remembered that the light fittings up here were old and rusty, and that Colin hadn't wanted to risk putting bulbs in them until they had been replaced.

Feeling a little nervous, Bridget leaned in and looked left and right. The long, low room was full of shadows that seemed as thick as dust. At the far end Bridget could just make out Colin's desk. A reading lamp was standing on it. To check out the room fully she would have to walk a dozen or so steps across to the lamp and turn it on.

She took a deep breath, and then wished she hadn't. The dust made her cough. Here we go, she thought, and marched towards the desk. She was half-way across the room when something on the seat of the chair that was tucked under the desk shifted and rustled. Bridget stopped, staring into the shadows.

It was so dark that she couldn't be sure, but it looked as though something spindly and ragged was rising slowly over the back of the chair. Bridget heard scratching sounds, like old twigs rubbing together. Slowly she began to back away, towards the door.

It was only when the thing fell from the chair to the floor with a clatter that Bridget turned and ran. In the few seconds it took her to reach the door and slam it behind her, she thought she could hear the thing scuttling after her. She ran down three flights of stairs, across the hall-way and out of the front door, stopping only to grab her bag from the hall table.

When she closed the door and turned to face the night, she saw that there were things moving in the front garden.

"No," Bridget moaned, and ran across to her car. She rooted round in her bag for her keys, and thought for one horrible moment that they weren't there. Then she found them and fumbled them out. With fingers that felt fat and numb she pressed the button to unlock the car.

She tore the car door open, jumped inside, then slammed and locked it behind her. Shaking with fear, she jammed in the keys and turned on the engine. Only then did she allow herself to look again at what she had seen.

There were shapes moving at the bases of the three stumps in the front garden. They were struggling feebly, as if the earth was giving birth to them. Bridget tried to tell herself that they were hedge-hogs or foxes or badgers, but she knew that they weren't. Although it was dark, the moving shapes looked to be made of twigs and roots and black earth.

Trying to stay calm, Bridget put the car into gear and drove away from the house. It was only a mile or so down the road, when she knew she was safe, that she started to sob.

Chapter 11
Ashes

Bridget didn't go to Claire's house because she didn't want Ellie and Miles to see the state she was in. Instead she drove until she found an all-night café and pulled into the car park. From there she called Ruth on her mobile. Ruth was groggy with sleep, but promised to drive over straight away. Bridget told her exactly where she was and then lay down across the front seats of the car.

She couldn't remember ever feeling more exhausted. The lack of sleep over the past two nights, along with everything she had been through, had really taken it out of her. She closed her eyes and within seconds had fallen into a deep sleep. She woke up two hours later to the sound of Ruth banging hard on the driver's window.

"I was getting worried," Ruth said when Bridget opened the door. "I've been hammering away for the last ten minutes."

Bridget had no energy to reply. She didn't feel as though the sleep had done her any good at all. Her body still felt as if it was being dragged down by heavy weights.

"God, you look awful," Ruth said. "Come on, let's go in the café. You need a hot, strong cup of tea and something to eat."

The café was bright with strip lighting, which reflected off the formica furniture and hurt Bridget's eyes. The only other customer was a trucker, a giant of a man with a bushy black beard and tattooes down his arms.

Ruth ordered tea and toast for two, and then asked Bridget what had happened. Bridget told her story slowly in a low voice. She stopped now and then to sip her tea or take a bite of toast. Ruth listened to her silently.

When Bridget had finished, Ruth reached out and took her hand. "You know what we have to do now, don't you?"

"What?" said Bridget.

"We have to go back to the house and look around."

Bridget shrank back. "I don't know if I can."

"We *have* to, Bridget," Ruth said. "You can't stay away for ever, you know."

They went in Ruth's car. Ruth fussed around Bridget as if she was a sick child. She strapped her in and put a blanket over her knees. Bridget closed her eyes, and within seconds was asleep again.

She heard a voice say, "Bridget, we're here." She thought she was dreaming until she felt herself being shaken awake. She opened her eyes. She was sitting in a car in her own drive-way. Then it all came flooding back, and her head snapped around to look at the stumps in the front garden.

The ground around their bases didn't seem to have been disturbed. There was nothing to suggest that anything had burrowed its way up through the soil.

"So far, so good," Ruth said. "Shall we go inside?"

Bridget looked at the house. In the early morning light it looked still and peaceful. Even so, it made her shiver.

"I don't know if I can," she said.

Ruth sat for a moment, looking at her friend. Then she said, "OK, do you want to wait here while I go in and look around? I don't mind."

Bridget didn't know what was worse – the thought of being left here or the thought of Ruth creeping around the house on her own.

"No," she said. "We go together."

"Come on, then," Ruth said.

They got out of the car and went into the house. Nothing seemed out of place, and the only sound they could hear was the faint music of bird-song from outside. They moved from room to room, just as Bridget had done last night. At last they were standing at the foot of the stairs leading up to the attic.

Ruth looked at her friend. "Are you OK?"

"A bit nervous," Bridget admitted.

"Do you want to wait here while I go up?" Ruth asked.

Bridget thought of Ruth opening the attic door, and then something reaching out with long claws and yanking her inside.

"No," she said, "we'll go up together."

They crept up the stairs, which creaked beneath their weight. At the top Ruth put her ear to the door, and then she pushed it open.

"That's weird," she said.

"What is?" asked Bridget with fear in her voice.

Ruth moved into the room. "See for yourself."

In the daylight the attic looked almost cosy. A band of sun-shine slanted in through the sky-light, giving everything a soft, warm glow. Ruth stepped forward and bent down to examine something on the floor. In the shadowy light it looked to Bridget as if a strip of the wooden floor, from the desk to the door, was charred.

"What is it?" she asked.

Ruth looked up at her. "I think it's ashes."

She was right. It looked as though someone had scooped ashes and chunks of burnt wood out of the fire-place downstairs and scattered them in a line across the floor.

She thought of the thing scuttling after her in the dark last night, but she still asked, "Why are they here?"

Ruth looked at her. "You tell me," she said.

Chapter 12
Jean's Story

After they had checked the house, Bridget went to bed and slept for the next ten hours. She woke up at six pm, and went downstairs to find Ruth, Ellie and Miles eating pizza and chips in the kitchen.

"I've made up my mind," Bridget said, as if she had been thinking all day instead of sleeping. "I'm going to ring Claire and see if she'll take me to see Jean Brook. I want to try and get to the bottom of what's going on."

Less than an hour later Bridget was sitting in Claire's car outside Jean's little cottage. In that time she had taken a shower, dressed and rung the hospital to check on Colin, and she was feeling more like her old self.

Jean's cottage was painted white and had roses growing around the front door. Before they got out of the car, Claire turned to Bridget with a worried look on her face.

"Jean's frail and a bit forgetful," she said. "I wouldn't expect too much."

"Don't worry," Bridget replied. "I'm not going to bully her. Anything she can tell me about the stumps will be useful."

They walked down the path and knocked on the front door. Their knock was answered by a mouse of a woman wearing glasses, and with a powder puff of white hair.

"Hello, Jean," Claire said. "I phoned to say we were coming."

"I know you did, dear," Jean said with a smile. "I'm not senile yet, you know."

She ushered them in and showed them through to the sitting room. The room was full of huge items of dark furniture, including a side-board which almost filled the back wall, and a grandfather clock whose top was only an inch or so beneath the ceiling.

Until two years ago the old lady had lived in the Morgans' new house. Bridget thought that all this heavy old furniture must have looked fine there, in the big, tall rooms, but here it just made the house look cramped and dark.

Claire introduced Bridget, and then poured three cups of tea from a pot that Jean had prepared for their arrival. She chatted with the old lady for a few minutes, giving Bridget the chance to look around.

She was hoping to see a picture of Jean's husband, Harry, and she spotted one almost straight away. It was on the mantelpiece, a framed black and white photograph of Harry and Jean on their wedding day, sixty years before. Jean was pretty and smiling. Harry was thin with dark hair covered in so much oil that you could see the comb-strokes in it. He was wearing an old-fashioned suit with wide lapels and he was grinning. He looked normal. Nice, even. It was hard to believe that this smiling man used to beat up his wife and lust after young girls.

"So, dear," Jean said, breaking into Bridget's thoughts, "how are you settling into my old home?"

Bridget looked at Claire and said, "To be honest we've been having a few problems."

"Oh, dear," said Jean. "Why's that?"

"Bridget's husband, Colin, is in hospital," Claire explained.

"Oh, I *am* sorry," the old lady said. "Is he ill?"

"We're not sure," replied Bridget. "He's having some tests. He's not been well since he touched one of the wooden stumps in the garden. I was wondering if you could tell me what they were, Jean?"

For a moment Jean was silent – and then Bridget was alarmed to see tears running down the old lady's cheeks.

Claire said, "Are you all right, Jean?"

Jean dabbed at her eyes with a tissue.

"Ignore me," she said. "I'm being silly."

"I'm sorry if I upset you," said Bridget.

Jean waved a hand. "No, no, dear, it's not your fault. It's just that it was hard to leave my children. I try not to think about it most of the time."

Bridget and Claire looked at each other in surprise. "Your children?" said Claire.

"Do you mean the stumps, Jean?" Bridget asked. "The wooden stumps all around the house?"

Jean sniffed and nodded. "I didn't want to leave them," she said. "I'm not a bad mother.

But I couldn't cope in that big house on my own after Harry died. You do understand, don't you?"

Bridget *didn't* really understand, but she nodded. "Of course we do," she said.

Jean leaned forward. All at once she had an eager look on her face. "Tell me, dear," she said, "are my children happy?"

For a moment Bridget didn't know what to say. Then she saw Claire give a little nod.

"Yes," she said to the old lady, "they're very happy."

"Oh, I'm *so* glad," said Jean, sitting back with a smile. "I couldn't bear the thought of them being miserable."

Bridget asked, "Where did your children come from, Jean? Who made them?"

Jean looked surprised. "Well, Harry and I did, of course," she said. She leaned forward and added in a whisper, "In the normal way."

This time Bridget *really* didn't know what to say. There was a short silence, and then Claire said, "Well, it's been lovely to see you, Jean. Thank you for the tea."

Bridget and Claire stood up and the old lady showed them to the door.

Just as she was about to step outside, Bridget turned back to Jean and asked, "Your children aren't ... well, *dangerous*, are they, Jean?"

Jean laughed. "Of course not, dear," she said. "They're all as sweet as lambs. Not a single one of them would even hurt a fly."

Chapter 13
The Attack

Bridget had been gone for three hours. Ruth was sitting on the settee, watching TV and drinking a glass of wine, when she heard the front door open.

"Bridget?" she called. There was no reply. She called her friend's name again, and then she went out into the hall-way.

The front door was standing wide open. "Bridget?" Ruth called for a third time. Then she heard thumping sounds coming from upstairs.

Something was wrong. Ruth didn't know *how* she knew, she just knew. She tried to shout out the names of the children, but her throat suddenly felt too tight. She ran up the stairs.

The thumping sounds were coming from Miles's room. She could hear another sound now too, a sort of choking, gurgling sound. She ran into the room and turned the light on.

Miles was lying on the bed and Colin was sitting on top of him. Colin had his hands around his son's throat and was trying to strangle him. Ruth stared in horror at Miles's purple face and swollen eyes, and then she screeched and threw herself across the room. She hit Colin like a battering ram. She grabbed his right arm and tore his hand from Miles's throat.

Colin tried to shove her away, but Ruth was set on getting him away from Miles. She punched him and raked at his face with her finger-nails, and at last he was forced to let go.

"You stupid bitch!" Colin snarled. "He's trying to sneak his way back in. Can't you see that?"

Ruth glared at him. He looked utterly mad. "That's your son!" she screamed at him. "That's Miles!"

Colin shook his head. "It's a trick," he said. Then his face changed. He looked suddenly sly. "But you know that, don't you? You want him here."

Before Ruth could answer, there was a scream from the door-way. Ellie was standing there in a pair of red pyjamas.

"Dad, what are you doing?" she wailed.

Colin looked at his daughter. For a moment he looked guilty and confused. Then he gave a cry, swept Ruth out of his way and ran from the room.

Ellie stepped aside as he passed. Then she said, "Ruth, what's going on?"

Ruth was already at Miles's side, checking him over. "He tried to strangle Miles."

"Oh, God!" cried Ellie, and put her hands to her face. "Is he dead?"

There were bruises around Miles's throat, but his face was returning to its normal colour and his eyes were fluttering.

"No," Ruth said, "he's not dead. He'll be fine."

Suddenly there was another person in the doorway. It was Bridget. "What's happened?" she said.

Ruth was shaking now, but she forced herself to stay calm. "Colin was here. He tried to strangle Miles. I was able to fight him off."

Bridget ran across to her son. She looked in horror at the bruises on his throat. "Where's Colin now?" she said.

"I don't know," Ruth said. "He ran away."

Bridget kissed her son on his forehead. Then she stood up and said, "Ruth, will you take Miles to the hospital? Ellie, you go too."

"What are you going to do?" asked Ruth.

"I'm going after Colin," Bridget replied.

Ruth looked horrified. "Bridget, you can't."

"Yes, I can," Bridget said.

"But Colin's not himself. He's dangerous," said Ruth.

"He won't hurt me," Bridget said firmly.

"But ... but you don't know where he is," Ruth said.

"I've got a pretty good idea," said Bridget. She reached out and touched Ellie's cheek. "Just get Miles to the hospital," she said. "I'll see you soon."

Then she was gone.

Chapter 14

Rain

Bridget tramped through the corn field, shining her torch in front of her. Small creatures scurried away from the light. The trampled corn stalks looked dry and brittle. They crackled under-foot like dry twigs.

"Colin," Bridget called, "are you there?"

There was no reply, but something told Bridget that Colin had come this way. She felt that the key to everything lay in the woods up ahead.

She found the place where she had entered the woods two nights ago and stepped into the trees. She shone her torch left and right. Tree trunks loomed out of the darkness, yellow and sickly.

She checked her watch so that she wouldn't lose track of time and started walking. Every few minutes she stopped, shone her torch around, and called Colin's name. Now and then she heard rustling in the bushes, but they were small sounds that couldn't have been made by anything bigger than mice or rabbits.

After twenty minutes she shouted, "Colin, it's me, Bridget. If you're there, please come out. I'm worried about you. I just want to talk."

This time she was answered by a tiny 'tap' of movement. She shone her torch towards the sound. But then another tap came from behind her. And then another, over to her left.

It was rain. For the first time in weeks it was raining. Bridget shone her torch upwards and saw it coming down from the sky, reflecting the light like glittering jewels. She felt a dash of wetness on her cheek as it started to rain harder, patting the leaves and the ground.

Bridget wondered what to do. Should she go on or turn back? She made up her mind to walk a little further. She set off, the muddy ground already becoming boggy under-foot.

After five minutes she stopped again. It was raining hard now. Her wet hair was plastered to her head. What was worse was that the torch-light was not as bright as it had been when she had set off. The batteries were failing. The last thing Bridget wanted was to be stuck out here in the dark like last night.

She thought she should turn back. But before doing so, she shouted Colin's name and swept the torch around one last time.

Something flashed to her right as the torch beam swept over it. It was at ground level, and all she could see from here was a thin sliver of light, as if someone had stuck a piece of broken glass into the earth. She moved forward, and as she got closer to the object she became aware that there was more than one of them. At least ten long metal objects were reflecting her torch-light back at her.

With a shock, Bridget suddenly understood what the objects were. They were knives! And what was more, they were *her* knives, the ones that had gone missing from the kitchen. Someone had brought them into the woods and stuck them into the ground. Or rather, they had stuck them into something *in* the ground, something that was lying in a six-foot-long hollow beside a mound of earth.

Bridget took two steps closer. Now she was able to shine her torch straight into the hollow. In the yellow beam she saw a body, brown and withered. The eye sockets and the wide-open mouth were packed with mud. Bridget's kitchen knives were sticking out of its chest, legs, arms and throat, as if to pin it to the ground in which it lay.

Bridget staggered back, too horrified even to scream. She dropped the torch, which hit the ground and went out, leaving her in darkness. She turned away from the grave and began to run back the way she had come. She slipped and stumbled in the mud. Branches whipped at her face. The rain beat down on her head.

Something flashed in the trees to her right. It was the disc of a torch beam, and it was coming towards her. The man holding the torch shouted something, but the rain drowned out his words. Bridget turned and ran the other way. She felt like a hunted animal, exhausted and terrified and plastered in mud.

After a couple of minutes she looked behind her. There was no sign of the man's torch-light now. She ran on – and suddenly a circle of light appeared right in front of her and shone directly into her face.

Blinded by the light, Bridget skidded and fell. Before she could get to her feet, a figure loomed over her and a hand closed around her arm.

Chapter 15
Questions

Ruth had called the police and they had found Bridget in the woods. But they had found a man's body too, lying in a shallow grave with a dozen kitchen knives sticking out of it.

The police hadn't told Ruth much, but WPC Summers, the female officer who had been ordered to stay with the two women at the house, *had* let it slip that the man had not died as a result of being stabbed by the knives. It seemed his body had been buried in the woods for at least six months, whereas Bridget and Colin had brought the knives with them when they had moved into their new home less than two weeks ago.

Ruth was now sitting with Bridget in the front room. Bridget hadn't said much. WPC Summers had told Ruth that Bridget was in shock, and that Ruth shouldn't ask her any questions for the time being.

Dozens of police were now searching the woods and the local area, but they hadn't found Colin. At least the children were OK, thought Ruth. Miles was in hospital, recovering well, and Ellie was once again spending the night with Bridget's neighbours, Tom and Claire.

Two hours had now passed since Bridget had been brought back to the house. Most of that time had passed in silence. When there was a knock at the front door, Bridget looked up and said, "Colin." It was the first word she had spoken for twenty minutes.

It wasn't Colin, though. It was a policeman with a thin face and grey hair. He was wearing a bulky black jacket shiny with rain. He entered the room with WPC Summers.

"This is Sergeant Brand," WPC Summers said. "He'd like to ask you a few questions, Bridget."

Sergeant Brand sat down. Bridget stared at him. In a soft voice he said, "I'm going to say a name, Bridget, and I want you to tell me whether you've heard it before. Can you do that?"

Bridget nodded.

"OK," the policeman said. "The name is Jason Riley."

"Oh, my God," said Ruth, and put a hand to her mouth.

Sergeant Brand looked at her.

Then Bridget said in a dull voice, "Yes, I know Jason."

"What can you tell me about him, Bridget?" Sergeant Brand asked.

"I used to work with him," Bridget said. "We were friends."

Brand frowned. "Where did you work with him?"

"In Leeds," said Bridget, "at the fitness centre."

Ruth saw Sergeant Brand and WPC Summers exchange a quick look. She wondered if Bridget had guessed why the policeman was asking her questions about Jason.

"When was the last time you saw Jason Riley, Bridget?" Brand asked.

Bridget shrugged. "Over a year ago. He went away. We're not friends any more."

"I see," said Brand, but Bridget slowly shook her head.

"I don't think you do," she said. And then she surprised Ruth by saying, "Jason's dead, isn't he? It was his body I found in the woods, wasn't it?"

Sergeant Brand was silent for a moment, and then he nodded. "It hasn't been confirmed, but we have reason to suspect so, yes."

Bridget sighed, but her face was set, mask-like.

"And it was Colin who killed him, wasn't it?" she said.

Chapter 16
Answers

Bridget told the police everything. She told them about her marriage problems, about her affair with Jason, and about how Jason had written a letter resigning from his job and then had seemed to vanish from the face of the earth. She told them about how she, Colin and the children had moved here to make a fresh start, and about Colin's odd behaviour since they had arrived.

Bit by bit the pieces of the jigsaw were coming together. After Sergeant Brand had gone, Bridget, Ruth and WPC Summers sat and talked it all through, trying to fit the missing pieces into place.

Bridget did most of the talking. She spoke in a low, calm voice, but to Ruth she still seemed not quite there. Ruth guessed that her best friend was still in shock and that the full impact of what she was saying wouldn't hit her for some time.

"When Colin found out about the affair he must have gone round to Jason's flat," Bridget said. "I'm sure he didn't mean to kill Jason, but somehow it happened. He must have brought Jason's body all the way down here and buried it in the wood. Then he wrote a letter of resignation, pretending it was from Jason, and sent it to the fitness centre. Maybe he wrote other letters too, to Jason's friends and family, saying he was going away. Maybe that's why no one came looking for him."

She fell silent for a moment, as if thinking about what she had said. Then she continued, "Do you know how we found this house? We found it because Colin got lost on the way to a job interview. It was just after he had found out about Jason, around the time that Jason vanished. When Colin got back from the interview he was more positive than I'd seen him in a long time. He said the interview had gone well, and that he had seen a house with a 'For Sale' sign outside it, and had fallen in love with it. He brought me and the children down to see it, and we all loved it too. It became something for us to aim for, the light at the end of our tunnel."

Ruth looked at her friend in horror. She wondered if Bridget knew exactly what she was saying. So Colin had killed his wife's lover, buried the body hundreds of miles away, and had then moved his family to within a mile of where the body was buried.

To Ruth that was the sign of someone with a very sick mind.

Maybe that should have been the end of it, but for some reason Colin had felt a need to go into the woods, dig up Jason Riley's body and pin it to the ground with knives.

Why had he done that? And then her eyes grew wide as it struck her.

"Oh, God," she said.

"What?" said WPC Summers.

But Ruth spoke to Bridget, not to the policewoman. "Colin thought that Jason was haunting him, didn't he?" she said. "He pinned him to the ground so that ..."

"So that he couldn't walk," Bridget said, nodding.

Ruth suddenly thought of what Colin had said after attacking his son: '*He's trying to sneak his way back in.*' Colin had been talking about Jason. He must have thought that the stumps in the garden were linked to Jason in some way, that somehow Jason had passed his spirit onto them. And then, when Miles touched one of the stumps, Colin must have thought that Jason's spirit had moved from the stump into his son. Which was why he had tried to strangle Miles. He had thought that Miles was Jason, come back to take revenge.

She opened her mouth to put her thoughts into words when suddenly there was a flare of light from outside, so bright that it was visible even through the thick red curtains at the window.

WPC Summers was the first to move. She ran to the window, pulled back the curtain and looked out.

"Oh, shit," she said, and a second later Ruth was by her side.

The stump nearest to the house in the back garden was on fire. Next to it was a leaping figure, his grinning face lit by the flames.

"That's Colin," Ruth said, and then both women turned as they heard a door slam behind them.

Bridget had left the room. They heard her running down the hall-way towards the kitchen. Ruth and WPC Summers went after her, the policewoman speaking into the radio clipped to her breast pocket, calling for back-up. By the time Ruth made it into the hall-way, Bridget was already in the kitchen, opening the back door.

"Bridget," Ruth shouted, "don't go out."

Bridget looked back. "He's my husband," she said. Then she slipped through the gap and was gone.

Ruth followed her, and was hit by a wall of heat. Both stumps in the garden were ablaze now. There was no sign of Colin, but Ruth turned just in time to see Bridget running around the side of the house. She and WPC Summers followed her, and as they reached the corner that led up the side of the house to the front garden, they saw that the stump here was on fire too.

To get past it they had to pass within a few feet of it. As Ruth edged by, she felt as if the flames were reaching out for her, eager to scorch her skin. She felt sweat spring out on her forehead. Then she was past. She ran to the end of the wall, round the corner and into the front garden, WPC Summers just a few steps behind.

Colin was in the front garden. He looked utterly crazed. He had already set two of the stumps here alight, and was shaking petrol on to the third from the big tin can that he held in his hand. When he had done that he lit a match and flung it at the stump. The petrol caught fire and the stump was suddenly coated in flame.

Bridget was moving across the lawn towards her husband, calling his name. Colin ignored her. It was as if he was aware of nothing but the burning stumps. He was laughing now, the sound high and shrill. The flames from the burning stumps reflected in his eyes, making them dance with fire.

Bridget stepped closer to her husband, reaching out her hands, but the heat from the flames was holding her back. WPC Summers pushed past Ruth and ran across to Bridget. She crashed into the back of her, bringing her down in a perfect rugby tackle. Both women fell to the wet, muddy ground. Bridget began to struggle, but Summers held her in an arm lock.

"Sorry, Bridget," the policewoman said, "but it's for your own good."

Because of the burning heat from the flames, Ruth had almost forgotten it was raining. She saw Colin raise his head and howl in victory at the night sky. Rain ran down his face. It plastered his hair to his head and his clothes to his body. Ruth stared at him, knowing he was beyond help, thinking how awful it would be for Bridget and the children to pick themselves up when all this was over.

Then she saw that something was happening *behind* Colin. There was movement at the base of each of the three burning stumps. At first Ruth thought that the stumps were beginning to split and blister. Then she saw that dark, burning shapes were breaking away from the stumps, standing up like small figures rising from a hunched position.

Now the shapes looked like burning children. Ruth could see their bulb-like heads and their black, stick-thin arms and legs. Colin had his back to the figures, and Bridget and WPC Summers were still rolling on the ground, so Ruth was the only one who could see them. She was the only one who saw them flow towards Colin. She was the only one who saw them pounce on him like a pack of wild dogs.

And suddenly Colin was on fire too. He was burning, like the 'children' that clung to him. Screaming in agony, he staggered about the garden. WPC Summers, sitting on Bridget's back, looked up and her face filled with horror.

Ruth ran over to her and shouted in her ear, "We need to get Bridget inside before she sees what's happened."

Summers nodded, and together the two women dragged Bridget to her feet and marched her towards the house. Bridget struggled feebly, but most of the fight had now gone out of her.

Ruth and WPC Summers led her through to the kitchen and sat her down. Bridget and the policewoman were coated in mud. All three women had sooty faces and stank of smoke.

All at once, thinking about what she had seen, Ruth felt sick and faint. She sank onto a chair and put her head in her hands. In the background she could hear the faint wail of sirens.

Chapter 17

Ghosts

Colin's funeral didn't take place until several weeks after he had died. Because of the murder inquiry, the police refused to release his body until they had finished with it.

By this time Bridget, Ellie and Miles had moved back up north, and were living with Bridget's parents while they looked for somewhere else to live. Bridget had not been able to face returning to the house in which she and Colin had hoped to make a fresh start, and so she had put it back on the market.

The funeral took place on a wet Wednesday afternoon in early August. It took place in Leeds, at Colin's parents' local church. After the service the guests were invited back to Colin's parents' house. Claire had driven all the way up to Leeds to pay her respects, leaving Tom at home to look after the children. Once the service was over and everyone was back at the house, eating the buffet which Colin's mother had prepared, Claire looked for Bridget's best friend, Ruth.

She introduced herself and then said, "Can I have a private word?"

The two women went out into the hall-way and found a quiet corner by the front door. "What is it?" asked Ruth.

Claire looked uneasy. "Well, I wanted Bridget to know something. To be honest, I'm not sure if it will help at all, but I think Bridget had a right to hear it."

"So why are you telling me?" Ruth asked.

Claire sighed. "Because now isn't the time to tell Bridget. I thought if I told you, you could choose a better moment – that's if you want to tell her at all."

Ruth took a sip of her wine as she thought about this. Then she nodded. "Go on."

"It's about the stumps," Claire said. "When Bridget and I went to see Jean Brook on the day that Colin died, she told us that the stumps were her children. I knew that Jean and her husband, Harry, had never had children, so I thought it was just a turn of phrase – you know, in the same way that some people say their pets are their children?

"Anyway, two days after Bridget and I went to see Jean, the old lady had a stroke. I got a call to say that she wanted to see me, and so I went to visit her in hospital.

"She was very upset. She told me she had heard about what had happened at the house and that she had something important to tell me. It turned out that although she and Harry had never had children, that didn't mean that Jean had never been pregnant.

"Jean told me that, in fact, she had fallen pregnant seven times, and she had had seven miscarriages. She said that no one had ever known about her pregnancies, and that she and Harry had buried their seven children in the garden. Under the stumps."

Ruth put a hand to her mouth. "Oh, my God," she said. "And Colin burnt them all. He burnt the graves of her children. No wonder the poor woman had a stroke."

"He didn't burn all of them," Claire said. "He died before he could get to the one on the far side of the house."

"Even so," said Ruth. "It must have been awful for Jean."

Claire nodded. Ruth looked at her as if she was weighing something up in her mind, and then she said, "Claire, do you believe in ghosts?"

Claire looked shocked. "What? I don't know. Why?"

"Because the night Colin died, I saw something," said Ruth. "Something I haven't told anyone about."

"What was it?" Claire asked.

For a moment it seemed as if Ruth was going to shake her head and tell her to forget it. But then she sighed, and told Claire what she had seen that night.

Claire listened in silence, and gave a shudder.

"What do you think?" Ruth asked.

Claire shook her head. "I think it's best to forget about it. Let the dead bury the dead." She looked at her watch. "I'd better be getting back. I've got a long journey ahead of me."

She said goodbye to Ruth, and asked her to pass on her love to Bridget and the children. Then she opened the front door and slipped outside. At the end of the path she turned back. She could see Bridget in the front room, talking to a tall man with a beaky nose and grey hair. Bridget looked tired and washed-out. She was flanked by her children, who looked older than their years, dressed in their funeral clothes. Even from this distance, Bridget could see the fading bruises on Miles's neck. Hoping that they would all be OK, Claire pushed open the gate and walked across the road to her car.

It was only then that she saw that her car boot was open. She hurried round to the back, thinking that someone must have broken into it. But if they had, it didn't look as if they had taken anything. Not that there was anything *worth* taking. The car boot contained a football, three pairs of muddy Wellington boots, a bin bag of old clothes for Oxfam and a box of newspapers for recycling. It also contained quite a lot of soil, which Claire thought must have leaked from one of the bags of compost she had bought at the garden centre yesterday.

And then she looked at the soil more closely, and realised it wasn't soil at all. It was ash and what looked like bits of charred wood, as if someone had cleared out a fire-place and dumped the contents in her boot. She frowned – and then she noticed that there was ash on the pavement too. Not only that, but there was a black trail of ash leading all the way across the road and right up to the gate of Colin's parents' house.

Strange, Claire thought. She checked her shoes to make sure she wasn't the one who had trailed ash across the road and into the house. But no, her shoes were fine.

With a shrug, she closed the boot, got into her car and drove away.

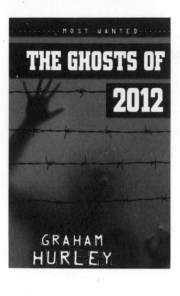

The Ghosts of 2012
by
Graham Hurley

Joe's on for gold at the 2012 Olympics. Nothing will stop him. He doesn't care that the army's taken over the UK. He doesn't care that anyone who stands up to the new government vanishes. All that matters is winning his race. But when Anna goes missing, Joe needs to know why. And what he finds will change the rules of the game. Forever...

Sawbones
by
Stuart MacBride

They call him Sawbones: a serial killer touring America kidnapping young women. The latest victim is Laura Jones – the daughter of one of New York's biggest gangsters. Laura's dad wants revenge – and he knows just the guys to get it. Sawbones has picked on the wrong family ...

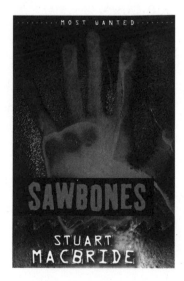

You can order these books directly from our website at
www.barringtonstoke.co.uk

No More Victims
by
Natasha Cooper

Ben was picked on at school. Now he's dead – stabbed in the street, and left to bleed to death.
The police are hunting the killer. Candy thinks she knows who did it, and she wants him sent down.
But what if Candy's wrong?

Kill Clock
by
Allan Guthrie

The kill clock is ticking ... Pearce's ex-girlfriend is back. She needs twenty grand before midnight. Or she's dead. She doesn't have the money. Nor does Pearce. And time's running out. Fast ...

You can order these books directly from our website at
www.barringtonstoke.co.uk